Library of Congress Cataloging-in-Publication Data

Day, Nancy Raines.
   Piecing earth and sky together; a creation story from the Mien tribe of Laos/adapted by Nancy Raines Day; illustrated by Genna Panzarella.
      p. cm.
   Summary: While she and her grandmother work on their embroidery, Mei Yoon listens to an old Mein tale about the creation of the earth and the sky.
      ISBN 1-885008-19-8
   [1. Creation—Folklore. 2. Yao (Southeast Asian people)—Folklore. 3. Folklore—Laos.]
   I. Panzarella, Genna, ill. II. Title.

PZ8.1.D3215Pi2001
398.2'089'9594—dc21   2001031348

Design & Production by Andrea Miles, Menagerie Design
Printed in China

Dedicated to;

American Women who began the project to create this book for the Mien people;
Barbara Emmons
Betsy Warwick
Ann Goldman

The beautiful models;
Chiaw Fin Saephan as Faam Koh
Mouang Fin Saephan as Faam Toh

And to the Mien people who bring their
culture and artistry and talents to America

PIECING EARTH & SKY TOGETHER

A Creation Story
from the Mien Tribe of Laos

Adapted by Nancy Raines Day
Illustrated by Genna Panzarella

Mei Yoon pricked her finger with the needle. "Embroidery is so hard, Grandmother." She dropped her work onto her lap. "And it takes so long. I'll never learn it."

Grandmother looked up from her stitching.
"Today is New Years, the first day of the whole year. We must make a good beginning."

"Couldn't I start by painting words like my brothers?" Mei Yoon asked.

"Someday it will be your task to make your family's clothes beautiful in the Mien way," the old woman responded.

"The job is hard and long, but when you're finished...."
Grandmother held up the panel she had just completed.

"Oh!" the girl gasped. "I could never make anything that fine."

"The harder you work, the bett[er] it gets." Grandmother's wrinkled face softened. "That reminds me of a story you might like to hear while we work."

Mei Yoon clapped her hands. "A story? What is it about?"

"A woman whose task was much bigger than yours or mine!" With that, Grandmothe[r] switched to her storytelling voice.

"In the beginning,
a helper from heaven
named Faam Koh
came down to make the sky.

His sister, Faam Toh,
came down to make the earth.

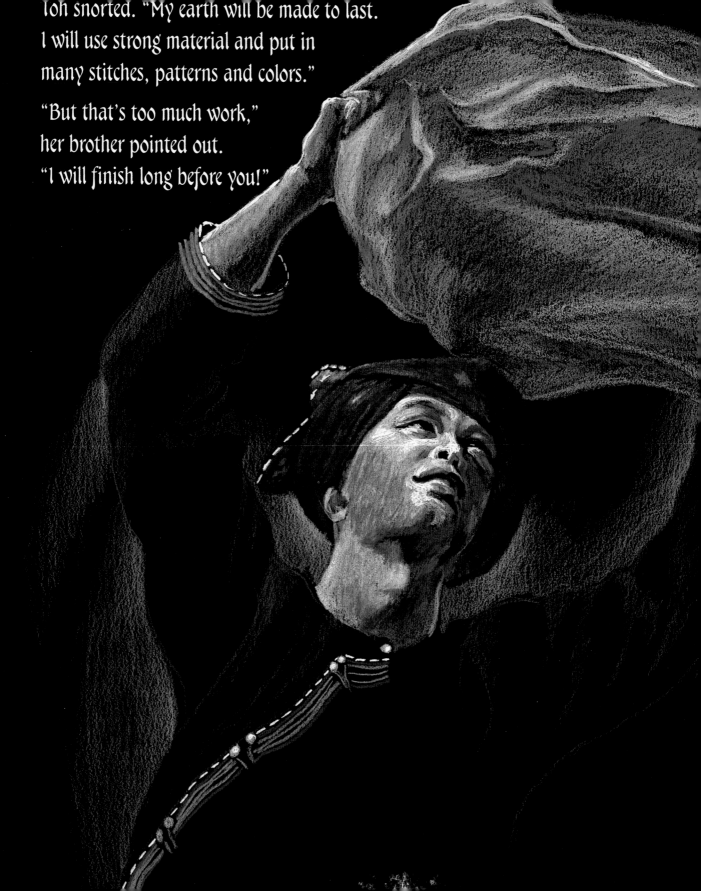

Toh snorted. "My earth will be made to last.
I will use strong material and put in
many stitches, patterns and colors."

"But that's too much work,"
her brother pointed out.
"I will finish long before you!"

"What does that matter?"
the sister retorted.
"My handiwork will be
far superior to yours."

Koh drew himself up tall.
"If this is to be a contest," he told her,
"I will work in secret."

Toh set her lips. "I will work in secret as well."

His back to his sister, Koh created the sky.
Then he fashioned the moon and stars to light
it by night, and the sun to light it by day.

He glanced over his shoulder.
"Do not look," he cautioned.

"Why would I want to?"
Toh sniffed.
"I am busy making the earth."

Masterfully, she blended rock and
soil into a quilt of textures.

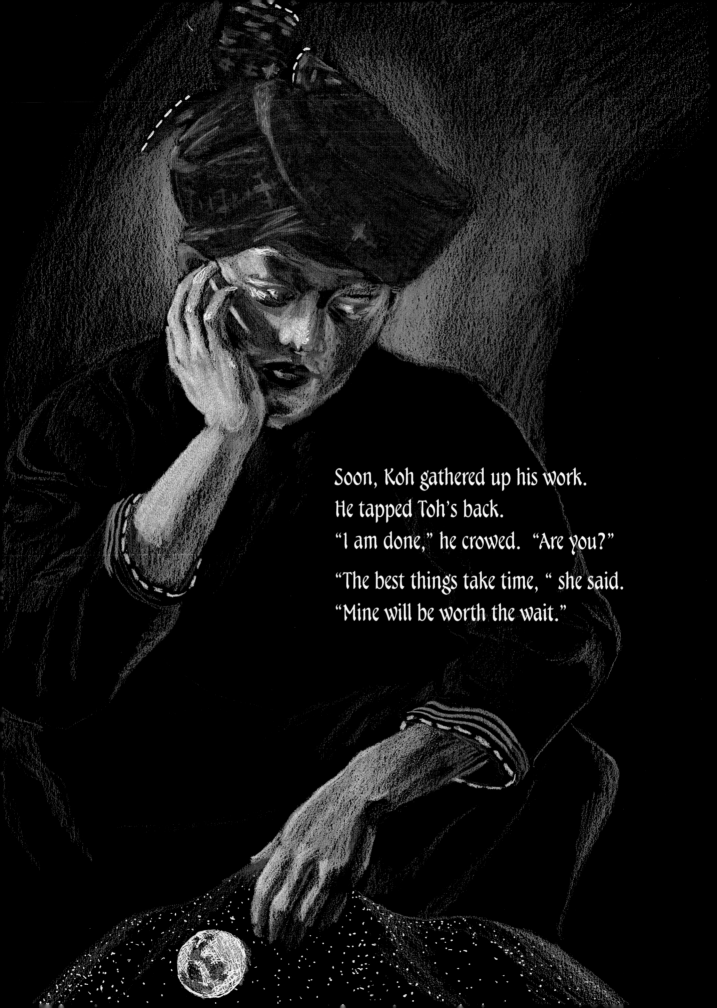

Soon, Koh gathered up his work.
He tapped Toh's back.
"I am done," he crowed. "Are you?"

"The best things take time, " she said.
"Mine will be worth the wait."

Koh sat down to wait. He drummed his fingers. He waited. He sighed. He waited some more. Finally, he lay down and fell fast asleep.

At long last, Toh shook his shoulder.
"Wake up, brother. I am done with my work.
But let me see yours first."

Koh showed off his sky.

His sister nodded.
"Your sky *is* lovely to look at."

"Let me see your earth," Koh urged.

So Toh unrolled...and unrolled her handiwork.

"Your work is fine indeed," her brother observed.
"It looks like a good match."

But when she held up her earth and he held up his sky, they did not fit together.

"Your earth is too big for my sky!" Koh shouted.

"Your sky is too small for my earth!"
his sister shouted back.

"Fine, then," said Koh. "I will make the sky bigger."

While his sister held one end,
he pulled and tugged at the other with all his might.

It stretched a little bit, and a little bit more.

Then it tore!

Its white, fluffy stuffing showed through the rips—the first clouds.

"Now see what you made me do!" Koh howled.

"Never mind," said his sister. "I have a plan."

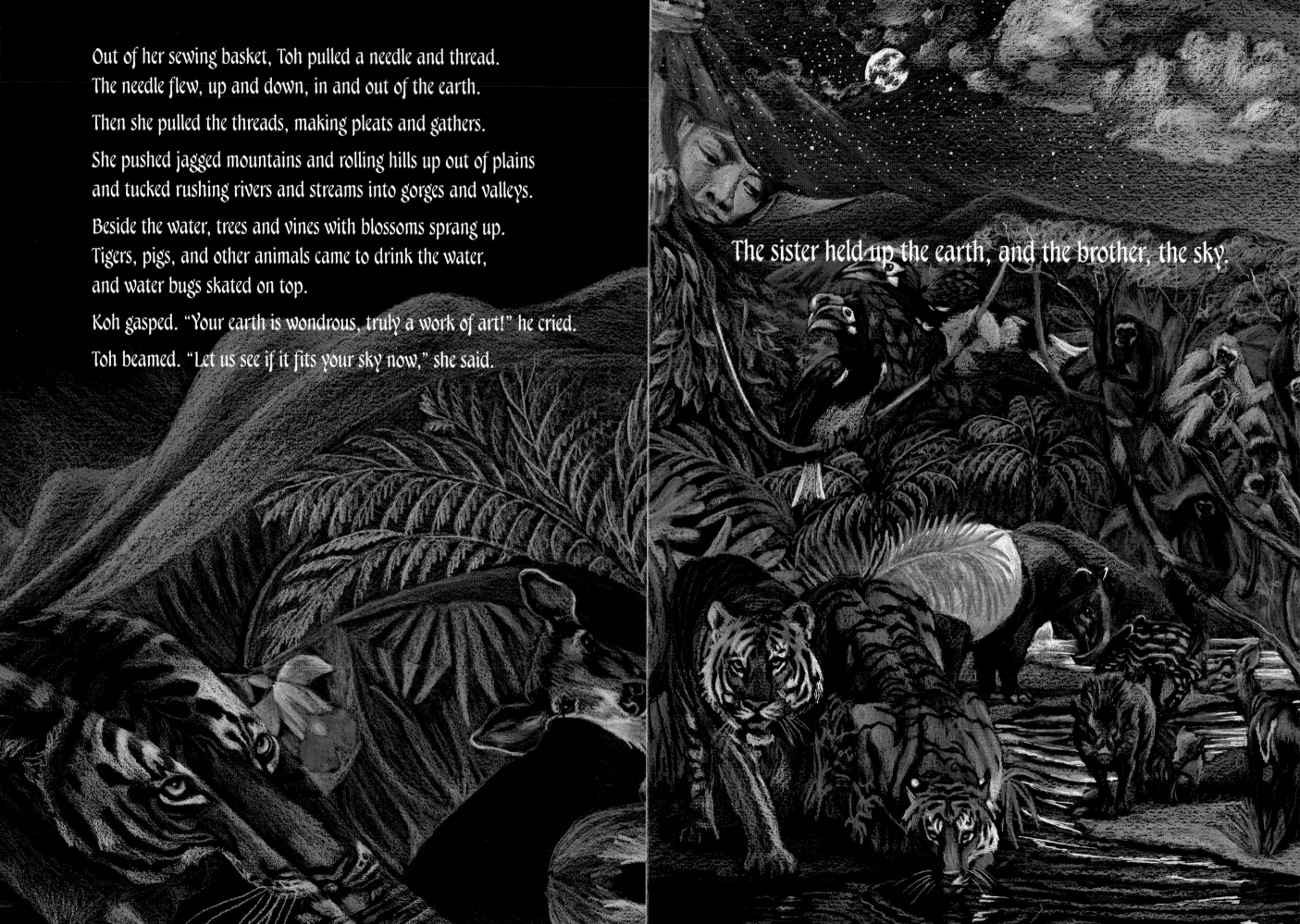

Out of her sewing basket, Toh pulled a needle and thread.
The needle flew, up and down, in and out of the earth.

Then she pulled the threads, making pleats and gathers.

She pushed jagged mountains and rolling hills up out of plains
and tucked rushing rivers and streams into gorges and valleys.

Beside the water, trees and vines with blossoms sprang up.
Tigers, pigs, and other animals came to drink the water,
and water bugs skated on top.

Koh gasped. "Your earth is wondrous, truly a work of art!" he cried.

Toh beamed. "Let us see if it fits your sky now," she said.

The sister held up the earth, and the brother, the sky.

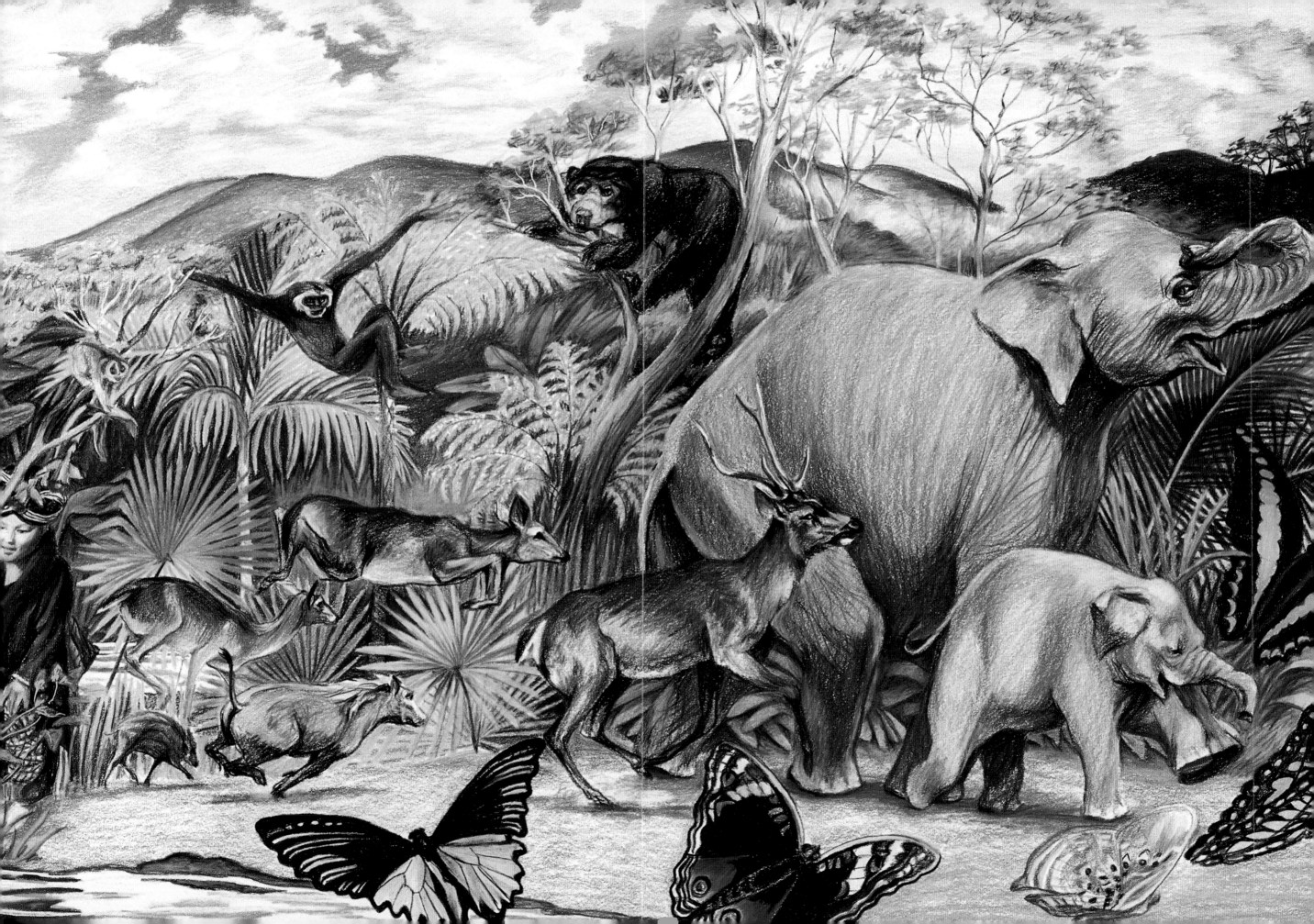

This time, they fit together exactly right.

Mei Yoon stopped her stitching and looked up with shining eyes.
"I like the way Toh figured out what to do."

Grandmother nodded. "Clever with her head and hands.
And takes the time to do it right."

"And see what I finished, Grandmother!"
Mei Yoon held up a sash, her very first handiwork.

The old woman's face crinkled into a smile. "A very good beginning."

Author's Note

In the highlands of northern Laos, the Mien tribe has passed down its distinctive embroidery for centuries. Girls as young as 4 or 5 start learning this art from their mothers or grandmothers, completing their first major project by age 9 or 10.

The Mien wear embroidered clothing every day—pants, long coats, sashes and turbans for women, sashes and jackets for men, and ornate hats and carriers for babies. Special clothing for weddings and religious ceremonies are elaborately embroidered as well. To make these clothes, Mien women use cotton cloth dyed dark blue or black. They count stitches carefully to create designs in weave, grid, or cross stitches. Designs reflect village life—many are named after animals; some, after crops or tools.

With so many projects to be done, girls and women always carry embroidery to work on in any spare time. Because cross stitches take longer, they did not become popular until Laotians had to leave their farms for refugee centers during the Vietnam War. Later, many Mien and other Laotians settled in the United States.

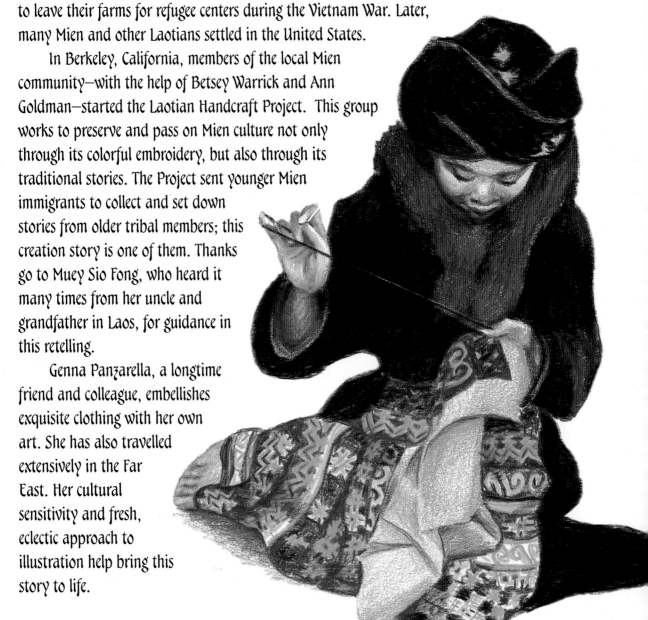

In Berkeley, California, members of the local Mien community—with the help of Betsey Warrick and Ann Goldman—started the Laotian Handcraft Project. This group works to preserve and pass on Mien culture not only through its colorful embroidery, but also through its traditional stories. The Project sent younger Mien immigrants to collect and set down stories from older tribal members; this creation story is one of them. Thanks go to Muey Sio Fong, who heard it many times from her uncle and grandfather in Laos, for guidance in this retelling.

Genna Panzarella, a longtime friend and colleague, embellishes exquisite clothing with her own art. She has also travelled extensively in the Far East. Her cultural sensitivity and fresh, eclectic approach to illustration help bring this story to life.

A Sampling of Traditional Mien Stitches

Scissor Handles

Spider

Water Bug

Tiger Claws

Gibbon (grid stitch)

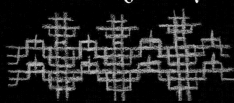

Tree Blocking Pathway

Pumpkin Blossom

Tiger Forehead

Gibbon (weave stitch)

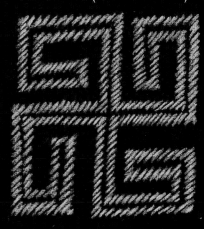

The Author & Illustrator

Nancy Raines Day is the author of *A Kitten's Year* and *The Lion's Whiskers: An Ethiopian Folktale,* a New York Times Notable Book. Ms. Day, who also teaches writing for children, resides in northern California with her husband.

Genna Panzarella is an artist and teacher living near San Francisco, where she and her husband raised their two sons. When she is not teaching or creating art, you will find Genna riding her horses. She also loves to travel and has been to South East Asia, as well as Africa, India, and China. Genna recieved her BFA at Washington State University, and studied for a year in Aix-en-Provence, France. Genna's artwork has explored many media, including fabrics, clothing, glass, oils, bronze, and even chalk drawing on sidewalks. This is her first children's book illustration.